We Want You
The Inside Story of The Nazi UFO

Michael X

Saucerian Publisher
Original Sources in Ufology

ISBN:978-1-955087-42-1

9 781955 087421

© 2023,Saucerian Publisher

Micheal X aka Michael Barton with his wife.

Prologue

Saucerian Publisher was founded with the mission of promoting books in Science Fiction. Our vision is to preserve the legacy of literary history by reprint editions of books which have already been exhausted or are difficult to obtain. Our goal is to help readers, educators and researchers by bringing back original publications that are difficult to find at reasonable price, while preserving the legacy of universal knowledge. This book is an authentic reproduction of the original printed text in shades of gray and may contain minor errors due to the aging of the pages. This title was originally published in 1960.

Michael Barton, aka Michael X. Barton adopted the pen name Michael X. to conceal his identity. In the mid-1950s, Michael Barton took a pilgrimage to Giant Rock. Inspired by George Van Tassel's apparent ability to channel ETs, Barton embraced the notion that the universe is composed of "mind stuff" that can transmit thought vibrations. On the historic night of May 22nd, 1955—his gaze fixed determinedly on Venus—Barton projected a "vibratory beam of light" and, using what he called "space telepathy". Based on his "closed contact" with aliens, he wrote: *Secrets of Higher Contact* in (1959).

In *We Want You,* published in 1960, Michael X explored the facet of Nazi-built UFO's. In the prologue of this book he concluded that: "But not all UFO's are true space ships. Not all come from outside -- or inside -- our planet Earth. Some of them are built on this Earth by secret forces on Earth. It now appears that "they" possess the secret of a POWER that may well be the key to the FATE of the world. That is why it is so vital that we learn something about "them" and their motives. THIS is the inside story of the Nazi UFO's." Michael X. The following SEVEN Chapters are contained in this book: Is Adolph Hitler Alive?, Escape to a Shangri-La, The Circle-Wing-Craft, Here is the Inside Story, His Hand Reaches Back, Who is Mr. Michalek?, UFO Surprise Package, The Third Slide You.

Editor
Saucerian Publisher, 2023

We Want You!

by

Michael X

THIS is an Educational and Inspirational Book of Study especially written and intended for NEW AGE individuals als everywhere. It contains Seven fascinating chapters. Statements in this Book are based on Scientific, Super sensory and Personal findings of the author. No claim is made as to what the information cited might do in any given case, and the Publishers assume no obligation for the opinions expressed or implied here by the author.

▲

Foreword

THE MYSTERY of UFO's -- Unidentified Flying Objects -- is the greatest mystery of our age, and it has many facets. Like a gigantic "jig-saw puzzle", the missing parts must be put into place in order for the picture to make complete sense. You and I are adventuring together and finding valuable missing parts along the roadside.

In this unusual adventure, we shall explore the facet of Nazi-built UFO's. Adolph Hitler, as we might suspect, enters the picture as a part of t he UFO mystery. Not all, but a definite part of it.

Michael Nostradamus, the French Seer, is also a part of this amazing drama, for he predicted that Hitler would escape from his enemies at the end of World War II. This event, as you will shortly see, has already happened. But more important to you and me and the world is the question: Will the Nazis return to the world scene in Earth-built UFO's?

Before we begin this great new adventure, Let me once again bolster your faith in the existence of INTERPLANETARY space ships and visitors from other planets. They are real. In space progress, some planets are far, far ahead of our little world. My conviction -- based on personal experiences -- is that our planet has had many visitations by highly evolved beings. They are still watching us.

But not all UFO's are true space ships. Not all come from outside -- or inside -- our planet Earth. Some of them are built on this Earth by secret forces on Earth. It now appears that "they" possess the secret of a POWER that may well be the key to the FATE of the world. That is why it is so vital that we learn something about "them" and their motives.

THIS is the inside story of the Nazi UFO's.

MICHAEL X

CHAPTER 1

Is Adolph Hitler Alive?

◆

SINCE 1951 I have been following with great interest, the working out of a strange and remarkable prediction. The Seer responsible for the prediction was a very gifted forecaster of future events -- Michael Nostradamus. The one about whom the "prediction" was made, and the subject of our story, is Adolph Hitler.

With uncanny power, Nostradamus could look far into future time by means of ESP -- Extra-Sensory Perception. What he saw happening in our own 20th Century is incredible and fascinating.

Nostradamus foresaw the advent of Adolph Hitler upon the world scene. In fact, the gifted Seer left certain verses for us to read, which clearly describe <u>Hitler</u>, the Nazi leader. But the most IMPORTANT prophetic verse of all -- regarding Hitler -- is the one that tells us how Adolph Hitler <u>escaped</u> <u>death.</u>

Here is this amazing event as Nostradamus saw it, and revealed it to mankind:

> "The leader who shall lead an in-
>   finite number of people,
> Far from their homeland to one of
>   strange manners and language,
> Five thousand in Candia and Thes-
>   saly finished,
> The leader escaping, shall be safe
>   in a barn on the sea. "

Notice that the above verse mentions the leader, or as Hitler was called, the Fuehrer, as <u>escaping.</u> The "barn on the sea" could easily mean a <u>submarine.</u>

To give us the idea more emphatically that it was a submarine that Hitler used for his escape from the Allies at the end of
World War II, Nostradamus wrote another verse:

> "Wild beasts for hunger shall swim
>   over the rivers,
>   Most of the land affected shall be
>   near the Danube.
>   Into an iron cage he shall cause the
>   great one to be drawn,
>   When the child of Germany shall
>   observe nothing."

Meaning? Could it be that Nostradamus was seeing in his
mind's eye a vision of proud and noble Germany beaten to her
knees in the closing days of the war? Here is the picture:

Berlin has fallen to the Allies. All is dark despair, hunger,
and hopelessness for the Germans. A report has gone out to the
people to the effect that Hitler, Eva Braun, Joseph Goebbels and
his family have all "committed suicide" -- are dead.

But was that report true? No. Nostradamus saw no suicide
of the Nazi leader nor of those who were with him in the Bunker
at Berlin during the final hours. If not suicide, then....what?

Escape. Get-away! How? By means of an "iron cage" -- a
submarine --in a manner so clever, so well planned that not even
the Germans themselves suspected! Adolph Hitler was alive!

Things are not always what they seem to be. If we let our-
selves judge only from "appearances" we are sure to be fooled.
According to the general report, it appeared that Hitler had died
by his own hand on May 1, 1945. I am convinced he did not,

I believe that Hitler escaped death...that he is alive today.
His purported "suicide" was not a fact, but a great hoax. Of
that we are quite certain. For the evidence you are about to read
is not based on mere conjectures but on indisputable facts.

Are you ready for bold adventure? Adventure of world-wide
importance in which we push back new frontiers? Then come...

First of all, it is important for us to realize that the assumed death of Adolph Hitler is something that neither the highest diplomat in America nor England nor Russia believes. Why? And why did Dwight D. Eisenhower publicly state on June 15th, 1945, that he had "grave doubts about the certainty" of Hitler's death?

Was it because of what American Intelligence officers failed to find in the "Fuehrerbunker" of Adolph Hitler? It was in this Bunker -- underground fortress of the Nazi Chancellory -- that the Allies searched for Hitler's remains. The story is this:

Hitler was supposed to have died of bullet wounds...death by suicide. His body was then supposedly doused with gasoline which was ignited so that the body was "cremated". The ashes? They were reportedly buried somewhere in the Chancellory yard.

But what are the facts?

Inside the Bunker the Americans found some blood stains but they were not of Hitler's type.

Outside in the garden, our intelligence technicians were just as unlucky. They found not a single bone, not even a tooth, no ashes, nothing that backed up in even the smallest way the story of Hitler's purported "suicide and cremation".

At once the Americans realized the glaring truth. Hitler's death was a great hoax...a lie. He had somehow staged the whole thing to fool his enemies. But his enemies were not fooled. Not the Americans. And if Marshal Zhukov, the conquering general from Russia, was fooled, his words didn't indicate it.

"The circumstances of Hitler's death," Zhukov stated, "are very mysterious. We have not identified the body of Hitler. I can say nothing about his fate. He could have flown away from Berlin at the very last moment. The condition of the runway would have allowed him to."

What did General Zhukov mean when he said that "very mysterious circumstances" were connected with Hitler's fate? At the official investigation carried out by Zhukov and his intelligence men, suspicious facts came to light.

When the Russians questioned the witnesses they had captured at the Bunker, the truth came out. The witnesses revealed that they had sworn to Hitler that if ever they fell into the hands of the enemy, they would maintain that they had seen his body and Eva Braun's body burning.

"In reality, " the Russians quote them as confessing, "We never saw either bodies or any live coals!"

The Russian investigators further stated that when their detachments came to the Chancellory garden on May 2, they found the charred bodies of Joseph Goebbels and his wife, and the burned bodies of their six children. They could find no trace of Hitler and Eva Braun. Nor did they locate any spot where they were supposed to have been cremated. One thing, however, was seen.

A jawbone with teeth. The Russians at once tried to locate Hitler's dentist. Oddly enough, both the dentist and his wife had completely disappeared. The "assistant dentist" identified the jawbone and teeth as "belonging to Hitler". But did it?

The jawbone could have been "planted" at the Bunker by the Nazis just before the Fuehrer made his escape. It is logical to assume that both the head dentist and his assistant were Nazis, and that the head dentist and his wife joined Hitler's get-away group. At any rate, they are still missing.

"We have established irrefutably, " the Russian report says, "that at dawn of April 30 a small plane carrying three men and a woman took off from the Tiergarten. Hitler's personal pilots -- Baur and Beetz -- have disappeared. Neither we nor the Americans have ever found them."

Another Russian commander echoed Zhukov. "We have found several bodies that might be Hitler's, but we cannot state that he is dead. My opinion is that Hitler has gone into hiding somewhere in Europe, possibly with General Franco."

Although it might seem obvious, Hitler could not have sought refuge in Europe. Much too risky. Neither could he have escaped

to one of the neutral countries such as Switzerland. Had any Government been so foolish as to provide a safe haven for Hitler, the act would have brought down the full wrath of the great powers upon it. It would have caused further bloody conflict, ending no doubt, in Hitler's capture.

We must bear in mind that Hitler was considered "World Criminal No. 1" by the Allied nations. Even under a disguise, some alert agent would have very quickly spotted him.

Frequently there have been rumors that German submarines, during their wartime travels to strange and remote places, had discovered an ideal refuge for the Fuehrer. There are tales about Hitler's "Castle on the Baltic", his "Fortress in the Rhineland", his "Monastery hide-out in Spain", his "Stronghold in Albania".

I have even heard a rumor that Hitler is being held a prisoner secretly by British intelligence on a small island off the coast of Scotland. The evidence, however, now indicates that all those stories are but wild tales. Yet Hitler did escape successfully.

Then where did he and his submarine convoy go in order to find a secure hiding place from which to resume activities, and plan future moves? It had to be away from the continent of Europe. And it could not be an island -- too tiny -- not enough growing room to expand into a large and powerful organized force.

Where did he go? Does any land exist where both climate and conditions for development are suitable? Does a land exist that is not overly populated and big enough to discourage enemies?

Yes, such a land exists. It is a big land, terribly big. It is located far from the continent of Europe. And its very remoteness makes it an ideal "haven of refuge" for Hitler and his group.

CHAPTER 2

Escape To a Shangri-La

———————●———————

In the previous chapter we had established a startling fact --
Adolph Hitler, leader of the Nazi Party in Germany -- did not die
in the Bunker when the Allies invaded Berlin in 1945. How then,
did he escape? And where did he go?

According to the prophecy of Nostradamus, Hitler used a submarine for his daring escape. Why then, did the Russian report
mention that a small plane had been seen taking off from the Tiergarten runway, in the cold dawn of April 30th? The answer to
this question is that Hitler made use of both the plane and the
submarine to accomplish his successful get-away.

At the Bunker where Hitler and his companions staged the big
hoax of "suicide and cremation", there were a number of underground passages leading in every direction. One of the passages
led to the vicinity of the airport runway.

In the Bunker with Hitler were Eva Braun, and four important
men of the Nazi Party. Martin Bormann (Hitler's right hand man
and brilliant organizer), Eric Kempa, General Von Greim, and
Joseph Goebbels with his wife and six children. They all escaped with the exception of Goebbels and his family.

Why did Goebbels die? There are two possibilities we may
consider. One: Goebbels and family might have escaped with
the others, and left doubles in their places. All the bodies when
found were charred beyond recognition. Two: Goebbels might
have turned traitor which could have caused the Nazis to shoot
him. There is good reason to believe this is so.

Although Joseph Goebbels was a genius at the art of propa-
ganda, he apparently had no real love for the German people.

Curt Riess, the writer who did a Biography of Goebbels, pointed out that "his contempt for the German people shocked fellow Nazis." And the Nazis weren't easily shocked!

But didn't Joseph Goebbels worship Hitler, and build up the prestige of the Fuehrer? Yes, at first. But Biographer Riess found that in the end Goebbels hated Hitler and even treated him as an imbecile instead of a God.

It is more than probable that Hitler and his entourage did not depend upon a single small plane to make their escape from the Bunker. Nor did they all leave on the same day. More than one get-away planes were no doubt employed by the escapees, and it is a good bet they left long before the "last minute".

The Nazi leader and his companions flew to a small port in Norway. It was there they kept a carefully planned "rendezvous" with a top-secret convoy of German U-boats. There -- sometime between April 22nd and May 2nd, 1945, -- Hitler and his aides embarked on the submarine that was to take them into the South Atlantic en route to a mystery destination.

The silent convoy of U-boats headed southward, following the "flagship" commanded by Admiral Karl Doenitz. It was his task to lead the convoy of submarines to the already prepared refuge which awaited them. Doneitz, in fact, had helped to plan the escape. He knew all about the secret "Shangri-La" Hideout.

When Hitler made his "last will and testament" he appointed the new German Nazi Government. Admiral Karl Doenitz was to become Reich President. Joseph Goebbels was to become Reich Chancellor, and Martin Bormann was to be Party Minister.

Most unusual! Why was Doenitz scheduled to become President of the Reich? Why not some politician, or Army general, or Airforce man? Why was a Navy man selected by Hitler?

Because Hitler was counting heavily upon Doenitz with his U-boats to assist him to escape alive from the danger area..and only an underwater submarine convoy could do this! U-boats in the German fleet were extremely difficult to detect, inasmuch as they traveled deeply submerged nearly all of the time.

ADMIRAL DOENITZ

Proof that Admiral Doenitz made the necessary arrangements by which Hitler escaped to a safe refuge, is not difficult to find. Doenitz, in the year 1943, let the "cat out of the bag" by saying: "The German submarine fleet is proud of having built for the Fuehrer in another part of the world, a Shangri-La on land, an impregnable fortress!"

The world quickly forgot this unusual statement by Doenitz in those hectic wartime days that followed. It was, however, most revealing. An impregnable fortress -- a Hideout -- had been built for Adolph Hitler in a land that was a veritable "Shangri-La"!

Where? South America -- tropical and warm -- huge in area and far enough away to discourage enemies, was the selected land. Argentina was the particular province that was chosen.

As early as 1948 it was suspected that Hitler had fled to Argentina in a submarine especially outfitted for that purpose. The Biographer, Curt Riess, in his book about Joseph Goebbels, was the first one (to my knowledge) to mention this astounding idea.

Two years later, in 1950, Gerald K. Smith backed up the big rumor. Speaking to a large audience at the University of Tulsa in Tulsa, Oklahoma, Smith not only claimed that Adolph Hitler was alive...but gave names of prominent persons who had seen and spoken to Hitler in Buenos Aires, Argentina!

In 1951-52, the editors of "The National Police Gazette" had gathered a mountain of evidence to the effect that the deposed Nazi leader was hiding in Argentina. A series of articles under the title: "Hitler Is Alive!" was published by that Magazine.

Those early articles told of the strange series of events that happened shortly after Hitler's supposed death. Unfortunately, back issues of The Police Gazette in which the full story appeared, are no longer obtainable. But here is the gist of it:

Strange but true, the German submarine U-530 had entered into the Argentine port of Mar del Plata on July 10, 1945. There it had surrendered to the Argentine officials.

Seven days later, on July 17, 1945, a second German sub entered Mar del Plata and also surrendered. It was identified as the U-977. The crew of both the U-530 and U-977 were questioned by the U.S. authorities, but the results of the questioning were never made public. They remain in the closed files of the Secret Service agencies, labeled, no doubt: TOP SECRET.

This strange fact is known. Both of the submarines contained surprisingly large food stores on board. There was a food supply sufficient enough to last for three, maybe four months at sea without restocking the larder. And both subs had been in the high seas for several months...on some unknown mission.

What were those submarines doing at Argentina? Why were they prowling around in the Atlantic even after the war ended? Clearly, they were part of the "mystery convoy" that transported Hitler, his aides and their personal valuables from war-wrecked Berlin to the new "Shangri-La" -- Argentina, South America!

"The Police Gazette" in December 1960, released to its reading public new, positive proof of Hitler's escape. The article was written by George McGrath, and titled : "HITLER IN ARGENTINA". It presents irrefutable new information on the Hitler mystery. By all means secure a copy of this new article in The Police Gazette at once...while they last. Address is : H. H. Roswell, Publisher, The National Police Gazette, 250 West 57th St., New York 19, N.Y. When you write, enclose a stamp, and ask how much the Dec. 1960 back issue will cost per copy.

In the above mentioned article, Mr. McGrath reports that he personally has examined documents in the files of Allied intelligence authorities. They confirm Hitler's escape. McGrath says that the startling new revelations about Hitler have been verified by the highest counter-espionage sources.

Adolph Hitler, then, is in Argentina. Why -- if that is so -- haven't the U.S. authorities gone in and captured him? For several very good reasons. For one thing, Argentina is known

to be "pro-Nazi". Former dictator Peron of Argentina was a very strong fascist and a good friend of Hitler. In fact, the Fuehrer has many friends and protectors in the Argentine government. By not cooperating with Allied intelligence agents, they shield him.

Then too, it is well-nigh impossible for any CIA (Central Intelligence Agency) men to get into Hitler's stronghold. Doenitz had boasted it was "an impregnable fortress". It is no doubt, exactly that. And according to McGrath's information, Hitler's "stronghold" is guarded by armed Germans.

The Hideout is located somewhere in "Patagonia". Patagonia is that area of Argentina where the Germans are particularly well-entrenched. Not only did the Nazis move their own people out of Germany, but millions of dollars as well. Fantastic as it may seem now, some $750 million dollars of Nazi wealth was funneled out of Germany into Argentina late in the war.

Using those funds, Admiral Doenitz and other top Nazis purchased many thousands of square miles of ranchland in Patagonia. The vast, sprawling acres known as "Pampas" were bought up and converted into the new, secret headquarters of the Nazis.

Aside from the fact that Hitler's Hideout is guarded by armed men, it would still be unwise for the Allies to attempt to capture Hitler and take him back for trial. His capture would undoubtedly lead to international complications of the most alarming kind... We shall soon see why this is so. Why Hitler is "too hot to handle". And why the U.S. makes no attempt to touch him now.

Please give your closest attention to what I am about to say. It is new and startling information. I ask you to keep this information in strictest confidence. It is for mature minds only.

LISTEN! Inside the "Sanctum Sanctorum" of the Hitler forces In Patagonia, what do you imagine you and I would find, if we were permitted to travel unmolested past the gates of the Hideout? Would we, dear friend, meet with the surprise of our lifetime ? Would we come upon certain underground installations - factories - staffed by German scientists ? There for what purpose?

To design, build and test what we would call "UFO's"!

CHAPTER 3

The Circle-Wing Craft

———•———

During the war the Nazis under Adolph Hitler authorized and carried out many secret military projects. Thousands of German scientists were set to work on these projects. This secret work was done at Peenemunde Island, Germany, and at other hidden centers underground. Two of these underground "factories" were located near Nordhaussen and Bleicherode, another at Traunstein, Germany. Each factory was given a secret "code name".

In charge of these secret projects were Professor Werner Von Braun, Professor Herman Oberth, and other missile experts. The designs for V-type rockets came from their drawing boards. For example, the V-1 and V-2 guided rockets which the Nazis used with such telling effect during the war.

SCHAUBERGER AND THE SILENT SAUCER

Now, dear friend, read on. For we are coming to a most significant "turn of events". Of all the secret inventions of World War II, by far the most exciting was the one that came out of Bad Ischl, Germany, as early as 1940. Around that time, a very brilliant engineer -- Vikton Schauberger -- was experimenting with Diamagnetism. That is, Schauberger was testing the attracting and repulsing properties of materials such as copper and various alloys. The results of his experiments were excellent.

Schauberger built model-size "saucer-shaped" craft for his tests. Some were bell-shaped, some hat-shaped. He powered them with an "Electro-Magnetic" engine.of his own design. By means of this new type of propulsion -- Electro-Magnetism -- The inventor succeeded in causing the disc-shaped models to fly silently through the air. And ... wonder of wonders ...the new Electro-Magnetic drive motor was flameless and smokeless!

Schaubergers Versuchsmodelle von fliegenden Scheiben aus Kupfer.
Gebaut im Jahre 1940 bei Fa. Kertl in Wien IV.

SCHAUBERGER'S EXPERIMENTAL MODEL OF A FLYING SAUCER
MADE FROM COPPER. BUILT IN 1940 BY KERTL CO. IN VIENNA..

In the June 1957 issue of URANUS, editor Egerton Sykes wrote:
"Engineer Vikton Schauberger of the Biological Institute of Bad
Ischl, well known for his 'Golden Plough' and his water purifica-
tion system, is reported to have produced and flown, as far back
as 1940, hat or bell-shaped craft -- presumably of model sizes --
made from copper utilizing diamagnetism. A reference to this is
in Mr. Sievers' book, Flying Saucers Over SouthAfrica."

Note that carefully..."produced and flown" in 1940. Where?
In Germany, and during the very time Adolph Hitler was in power.
We can safely assume that the Fuehrer's secret service agents --
who didn't miss a trick -- were fully aware of engineer Vikton
Schauberger's fabulous invention: the silent UFO.

(Above) In 1952, George J. Stock of Passaic, N.J., took five photos in sequence of same UFO as it passed over his home. Note force-field around the UFO. Also note striking resemblance to Schauberger craft shown in lower picture. It is "hat-shaped".

(Below) In 1940, Vikton Schauberger of Germany, built this "hat-shaped" model flying machine. It flew by "Electro-Magnetic" power which produced a force-field. Conclusion: UFO above could be a German-built device.

By 1943 Admiral Doenitz of the Nazi submarine fleet had not only located the ideal "Hideout" for the Fuehrer in far-off Patagonia, but had started furnishing that fortress lavishly. All the essential men, machines, buildings, laboratories, factories, tools, secret protective devices, everything Doenitz could find went into the "Shangri-La" Nazi project.

Including Vikton Schauberger's blueprints. Schauberger himself, did not leave Germany. But the plans for his invention of the "silent UFO" were far too precious to be overlooked by the Nazi secret agents. Doubtless they delivered a full set of the invention plans to the scientific technicians in Patagonia. As for the fate of Schauberger, I am told that he was set upon by mysterious assailants in 1952. He was badly injured in the chest and died three months later. A sad end for a genius.

Adolph Hitler always wanted "super-weapons". He knew that what he lacked in man-power he had to make up for by means of advanced science and technology. Prior to war's end in 1945, he pulled every conceivable string to get guided rocket missiles into production. He even had in mind a mammoth rocket -- the V-10 -- with a 5,000 mile range. And he had his eye on Schauberger's amazing invention. It required very little imagination to see how the Circle-Wing Craft, if perfectly silent and unbelievably fast, could be the means of winning the war.

Are you ready for more suprises? Good! Hold onto your hat because action gets more intense from here on.

In June, 1960, a German friend of mine -- whose name must remain confidential -- added another "missing part" to the great jig-saw puzzle. This friend stated that during the war he had acquaintance with Germans in East Prussia. They admitted to him that there were secret UNDERGROUND FACTORIES in the East Prussian forests, which produced key parts of the V-1 and V-2.

Not only that. Experiments were also made there on strange "ellipse-shaped" or "egg-shaped" metallic air-craft. In other words, Hitler was in possession of enough technical "know-how" regarding the new principle of propulsion (electro-magnetism) to apply it to crafts of several different designs. Now turn to the next page and my German friend will tell you of his experience:

HERE IS THE INSIDE STORY

"In Schramberg, South Bavaria I had a friend who's father was a renowned Metallurg scientist. He experimented with the chemistry of metals. There is little doubt but that he was one of the world's most brilliant minds, for it was this same scientist who invented <u>a</u> <u>metal</u> <u>harder</u> <u>than</u> <u>diamonds</u>. In 1935-36 the Nazis put this amazing metal -- we shall call it IMPERVIUM -- to use for the first time in airplanes of the German Air Force.

"I recall visiting his fantastic laboratories under a luxurious house at Lake Schramberg. He allowed me to see how the metal glowed with a red-blue florescence when heated to a high degree.

"One year later (in the 1940's) I met this scientist and his daughter again, this time at the Polish Embassy. The daughter told me that her father had been called for an audience with Hitler that very night. The scientist's consultation with Hitler concerned secret plans for an OVAL or 'ELLIPSE-SHAPED' aircraft!

<u>AUTHOR'S COMMENT</u>: From this data it appears the Nazis were definitely building an "egg-shaped" mystery ship, a top-secret UFO. Its source of power for flight ? Electro-magnetism or "electrified propulsion system". Its chassis built with heat-resistant metal: IMPERVIUM, the metal harder than diamonds!

I believe that manufacture of these "egg-shaped" UFO's and Circle-Wing Craft began in Germany's underground factories, but was moved to Argentina when military defeat appeared certain. How, one asks, could Hitler's Third Reich -- on the verge of collapse -- finance such a project? And in Argentina! Nothing is more costly than research and the manufacturing of strange, new types of secret flying machines in some far distant land!

★★★★★★★

CHAPTER 4

His Hand Reaches Back

◆

In 1942 the Fuehrer needed money and plenty of it. He needed money to research and develop "Super Weapons" with which to win the war. He needed money to expand his operations in South America, at the "Stronghold". He also required a large supply of money in case Germany lost the victory.

Hitler was advised that the quickest way to make money is to "make" money. During a war there is certainly no time to "earn" big money. It had to be "made-to-order" -- counterfeited.

The code name for this fantastic counterfeiting plan was "Operation Bernhard". Using this secret code name for their "money-making" operations, the Nazis manufactured $600,000,000 of British bank notes in World War II. This money was so perfectly counterfeited it was impossible to tell it from the genuine article.

"Operation Bernhard" is one of the most fascinating reports to come out of World War II. It is still labeled SECRET in the files of American, British, French and German intelligence agencies. INTERPOL which is the International Criminal Police Organization in Paris, has carbons of the report in its files. Operation Bernhard was big. Biggest in fact, of any counterfeiting activity of all time. And at the head of it was Adolph Hitler.

You can now learn all the inside details concerning Hitler's amazingly ingenious set up that turned out so much bogus British money...details which we have not space for here. It is all revealed in a small, paper-back pocket book entitled: MONEY OF THEIR OWN, by Murray Teigh Bloom. The book sells for 50¢. If your bookstore cannot supply you, a copy can be obtained direct from Ballantine Books, Inc., 101 Fifth Ave., New York 3, N.Y. I'm sure you would enjoy reading its fascinating facts.

One of those facts is that late in August of 1943, a leading member of the Nazi Party took $250,000,000 worth of the bogus bank notes with him to South America. There it was used, as we have previously mentioned, to "buy up" great tracts of land in Argentina, namely Patagonia.

Hitler's "Shangri-La" fortress cost money. Not only was it necessary to purchase land, it was also urgently required -- money that is -- to enable the German scientists to continue building the first working models of Hitler's "mystery weapons".

Money -- "made-to-Hitler's order" -- kept pouring into Patagonia via well established Nazi channels. The "impregnable fortress" became more and more luxuriously appointed. More important, progress on hhe secret UFO's (the Circle-Wing and Oval Shaped Craft) zoomed ahead. Hitler was optimistic.

But things were not going so well in Germany. 1944 saw things looking worse than ever before for the Nazis. By early 1945 they saw the "handwriting on the wall". Hitler's engineers had not managed to come up with the super weapons in time, and the Allies were preparing to storm Berlin. Hitler gave the order for a special run of the counterfeit money. Operation Bernhard in Berlin was to run off $10,000,000 (ten million dollars) of British pound notes. It was to be used by the Nazi leaders in Germany, as "getaway money"!

The special order got immediate attention. Result? Several thousands of top Nazis left Germany. The escape route was to Spain, and from there by boat to Argentina, South America.

Suddenly the war was over. The Allies had won, and it was taken for granted by the general public that the story of Adolph Hitler's "suicide" was true. It was not. Hitler was simply not the suicide kind of individual. Far from it!

Herr Keitel, the Nazi Chief of Staff, reported that the Fuehrer was something of a health fanatic. He went for a walk in the woods every morning while in his command post in the Black Forest. And how about Hitler's diet? It was strange indeed as compared with that of his fellow officers. Hitler did not eat meat. And it was widely known that he fasted from all solid foods at

least three successive days a month.

Now dear friend, considering the above, it is highly unlikely -- if not impossible -- that a man who looked after his physical condition to that degree would destroy himself. It is far more likely that Hitler -- who considered himself a man of Destiny -- would include himself in the Nazi getaway plans!

Hitler, far from being dead, is most probably very much alive. Quite naturally, he'd be older now...somewhere in his early seventies. But calendar years, we must remember, are not at all the important thing to one who "takes care of himself" properly. It's biological years, not calendar years that slow a man down.. make him weak and ineffectual. Right?

In my opinion -- take it for what it is worth to you -- I'd say Adolph Hitler is in good physical health today. I believe he has been diligently "planning big things" ever since he was forced to vacate Germany and flee to his "Shangri-La".

Those plans involve a resumption of power, obviously. But I think there is more to it than that. Hitler's birthdate was April 20, 1889. Those who know something of Astrology would say Hitler was born "on the cusp" between Aries and Taurus. That gives him a blending of qualities from both signs, Aries and Taurus. Result? Almost unbelievable boldness, daring, energetic drive. Such a person demands power, great power...yet has an uncanny ability to wield it. He can both gain and use POWER.

And here are the amazing facts. From his Hideout, the Fuehrer seems to be directing the rebirth of Nazi Germany. The hand of Hitler is reaching back . And it is beginning to touch and reorganize present-day modern Germany.

Germany today, as you know, is divided into West and East sectors. East Germany is controlled by the Russians, so it is in West Germany that Naziism is being "revived". Not that the West German Government approves. It is only too aware of what "Nazi tactics" (old style) may do again to the general citizenry. Hence it is fighting Nazi revival tooth and nail.

That has not fazed the Hitlerites. They have vowed to re-

build the Nazi Party from Argentina and keep alive the spirit of Hitler's Naziism. Martin Bormann, Hitler's top aide, has never been captured. Arrested yes. But never held for trial. It is his master-plan that has been operating ever since 1945 to organize a string of undercover Nazi units stretching from Patagonia all the way back to Germany the Fatherland.

World-wide secret societies are now busy in Germany, operated by Bormann's secret agents. To name a few, there is the "German Reichs Party", the "Socialist Reichs Party", and the "Freikorps Deutschland". All these are recently formed political organizations. The "Freikorps Deutschland" is pledged to overthrow democracy in Today's Germany. While none of these organizations call themselves "Nazi" -- that word is strictly "taboo" in Germany -- one simple fact stands out like a sore thumb: The members are all former Nazis or ardent Nazi supporters.

Anti-semitism (Jew hating) was a basic ingredient of Hitler's plan in World War II. Unless I am badly mistaken, it is still the basic ingredient of his followers today.

That is why some 30,000 Jews living in West Germany today are wondering what the future may hold for them. More than one incident has occured lately to unnerve them. For example, the sign of the "swastika" smeared on a synagogue...and upon the doors the order: "Jews, get out!" has been seen frequently.

In Berlin recently, 25 German students dressed up in the full regalia of Nazi storm troopers and paraded around Glienicke Park singing the same old Nazi songs that Hitler inspired.

In Los Angeles, California, on October 25, 1960, an unusual event took place. Four young "storm troopers" who objected to the mixed marriage of May Britt to Sammy Davis Jr., decided to "picket" the theatre in Hollywood where he was appearing. A half hour before the opening of the Davis show, the four would-be Nazis tried to put their "picketing plan" into action. They showed up wearing khaki shirts, black ties, and Nazi swastika armbands. Each man had a placard proclaiming "Pride in Race and Nation!"

The "plan" was a horrible flop. In fact, it turned out to be almost fatal for the four determined picketers. Before they could

do much picketing, some 100 theatre-goers and passersby took out their anger on the erstwhile "Nazis". The crowd screamed at the four youths, jeered at them and battered them severely about the face and head.

Police rescued the four young men from the crowd's fury, and after hearing their story, sent them home. It seems the defeated "Nazis" had been corresponding with the American Nazi Party in Arlington, Va., where they bought the arm bands for $1.50 each.

The youths explained that they were not "official" members of the Party because they haven't been able to come up with the required dues.

George Lincoln Rockwell is the self-proclaimed "Fuehrer" or leader of the American Nazi Party. He boasts a hard-core of 35 devoted followers at his headquarters in Arlington, Va. Anti-semitism is part of his "mission". It is doubtful that he knows the real Fuehrer is alive. But he continues to pass out the party's anti-Jewish handbills at every public meeting.

All of these undercover organizations serve one purpose... They weaken a nation, a government from within. It is the old Nazi technique of using "ideas" as weapons, namely, the ideas of "hate" and "fear". Back as far as 1920 Hitler had said: "Only by ideologically destroying it from within can Germany conquer Europe. By brute force alone, never!"

Watch out, dear friend, for the "Hate" and "Fear" groups in the cities where you live. These groups are so cleverly disguised with important sounding names, and so efficiently organized, it is often difficult to "smell them out". Watch out, too, for magazines or news publications that hammer out the HATE theme. Here, in plain words, is what they really want of you and me:

"WE WANT YOU to either hate or fear and to ACT from your hate or from your fear! Foment racial violence. Turn brother against brother. Turn your nation into a strife-torn, turmoil-ridden, starving and defenceless humanity. We will take it from there. We shall win. It is just a matter of time!"

CHAPTER 5

Who Is Mr. Michalek?

◆

The biggest mystery in German UFO circles from 1958 up to the present time, has been : <u>Who is Mr. Michalek?</u> Let me tell you the whole amazing story. I cannot promise to give you the final answer to the riddle -- for I myself do not know that -- but perhaps you can solve the riddle.

I hope so. Because there is apparently much more to the "Michalek Story" than appears on the surface. My job is to uncover as many related facts as possible regarding this highly mysterious personage known as Karl Michalek. I shall leave it up to you to "read between the lines" as the story unfolds.

Firstly, let me say this. Please do not confuse the name of "Michalek" with my own name (Michael X). They sound very much alike, I admit. But Michalek is definitely NOT Michael X (me), and I am definitely not Michalek.

Having settled that, we can go on with the story. It seems that in the year 1958, a mysterious individual by the name of Karl Michalek whose address was Santiago, Chile, South America, began to write some very unusual articles. He sent the unusual writings of his to a newspaper publisher in Germany. The publisher -- whose name was Louis Emrich -- printed everything that Michalek sent to him, and in an unbelievably short time "Michalek" had a large following of readers.

Louis Emrich's newspaper was called: "NEUES EUROPA" or in English, "NEW EUROPE". Until the advent of the articles by Mr. Michalek, the little newspaper presented a variety of different subjects to its readers. Then, all at once, from 1958 onward, the unique Michalek messages began to dominate the publication. The German readers were fascinated, intensely so.

With good reason. Michalek was calmly announcing in the "NEW EUROPE" that he -- Karl Michalek -- was in positive contact with the governmental heads of the planet Venus. The name of the particular intelligent being from Venus who was acting as Michalek's present contact, was "Ase".

Ase and Michalek are desirous, so said the articles, of bringing about everlasting peace and order to our planet Earth. In his series of regularly appearing articles, Karl Michalek presented himself to be a sincere, Godfearing man who believes in the almighty power of the Creator. He is against those world groups who are for promoting war, which Michalek knows will destroy this planet.

The book which you see pictured at the right, was published in Germany. Its cover says: MICHALEK, The Prophet Of The New Era. Unearthly Forces and the Human Race.

To get the facts about the big "Action-Program" of Michalek, let's turn now to an article which appeared in the "NEW EUROPE in May, 1960:   (Translated from the German)

MICHALEK AND HIS WORLD-WIDE ACTION PROGRAM.

"For almost 2000 years we have heard the glad tidings every year: PEACE ON EARTH! Unfortunately this glorious message full of blessings could not be put into realization by the nations because consuming strife was on a rampage everywhere, and a peaceful future was not in sight.

"The different nations -- always on the lookout to expand their countries and their wealth -- were for some time filled with

an awful quarrelsome egoism and always ready to swing the war-ax. Now a new, practical way has been found to abolish wars once and forever.

"The spiritual bearer of this great idealistic world idea is Karl Michalek, the President of the coming majestic government of the World Republic of this Earth.

"At the time of the crisis in Berlin at the end of March 1959, Michalek had advised Eisenhower and Khrushchev not to meddle in this conflict by force of weapons at all. If they did meddle in that manner, both Moscow and Washington would be wiped out.

"During the conference in Geneva in May 1959, Michalek sent a telegram to the four ministers in Geneva with the warning they were not to make any decisions which could lead to a third World War. Otherwise, the powers of Venus would see themselves as forced to bring the Earthly leaders to their senses by FORCE. In a note to the two great powers Michalek had explicitly demanded in July 1959 that all experiments with atom bombs should cease immediately.

"ULTIMATUM TO KRUSHCHEV: On March 12, 1960 Michalek put the Ultimatum to Khrushchev to withdraw the Russian weapons for mass destruction which were directed to other countries..... Otherwise he (Mr. K.) as well as all the members of his government would have to reckon with the most severe measures of punishment. (Namely, and invasion by the Venus fleet. M.X.)

"From this, one can see that Michalek is actively interceding in a confused, unsafe, abysmal world politic and wants to bring about an absolute peaceful handling of world politics. He alone could never have accomplished this. Who has been standing by him, and who has strengthened his backbone? The chief leadership of the planet Venus, who has the fullest confidence in him, has done this!

"He (Michalek) has been chosen by them to become the President of the coming nation-uniting World Republic of this Earth. He has also had several contacts and personal discussions with the leader of the proposed landing action, the Commander in Chief of the 3rd Venusian Space Fleet...Ase.

"With the announced New Order which is going to be established on this Earth, a new, more hopeful Age will begin in the world history...with the help and active support of the powers from Venus. Among other things it will bring the following important changes:

(1) Through the reorganization of the four continents --Europe, Africa, America, Asia -- all of the present existing States and nations will be declared Provinces. No boundaries will separate the States or countries, dividing the nations. There will only be Provincial boundaries.

(2) The earthly world republic will consist of 72 World-Provinces in the future.

(3) In all of the 72 World-Provinces capital punishment will be introduced for crimes like murder, robbery, arson, narcotics.

(4) Within the new earthly community of the nations a truly economical system will be established. The welfare of the entire humanity will depend upon the frictionless functioning of this economic system. All earthly nations shall be justly dealt with, and the world-wide hunger catastrophes which have become so permanent up to now, shall be abolished entirely.

(5) The whole system of finance will be put on an entirely new basis. A new monetary medium will be issued by the majestic government of the World Republic, which will have the same unified value in all the countries (Provinces) of this Earth.

(6) Nothing can be bought or paid for with the standard money which is being used now, after the Day of the Landing. On that Day the change to the new unit-money will be made.

(7) The existence of all colonial possessions will come to an end with the Day of the Landing.

(8) All military agencies and authorities will necessarily be dissolved in all the ex-States and world provinces within 30 days after the proclamation of the World Republic. Furthermore it is to be said: the people of the planet Venus do not want to conquer or exploit our Earth as our present earthly men of state would do

in a reverse case. But they are coming to save humanity of this Earth from atomic destruction which is inevitable should World War III come.

"FLYING SAUCERS have been sighted in more than a thousand cases, which sightings have been officially registered. Quite often they have landed on this Earth secretly and unobserved. A certain proof of this, is the fact that EXPERTS FROM VENUS have been living here on this Earth for the last 15 years. They speak English and German. (Note this. M.X.)

MICHALEK PREDICTS THE VENUS UFO LANDING!

At the beginning of his "career" Michalek -- for some strange reason -- decided to announce publicly in the "NEW EUROPE" publication, that "Der Tag X" (X-Day) was about to happen. A Landing of Venus Space ships would take place, said Michalek confidently, in the earth year 1958... on X-Day.

You can, I am sure, imagine the great excitement this bold prediction caused among Michalek's followers. In thrilled anticipation, everybody awaited "Der Tag X". On X-Day in December 1958, a whole fleet of Venus Space Ships would land in the city of Berlin, Germany, for all eyes to behold in awesome wonder.

December came...and went. No fleet from Venus showed up. In fact, to the bitter disappointment of readers of the "NEW EUROPE", there was not a single UFO anywhere to be seen.

What had happened? No one had the slightest notion, until Michalek explained. The chief leader of the people of the planet Venus -- said Michalek -- had passed away unexpectedly on December 17, 1958. The Venusian President, whose name was "Urun", had suddenly died at the age of 193. Ase, the Commander of the Third Space Fleet, saw himself forced to delay the landing maneuver for a short period of time.

Two years later, Michalek again predicted "Der Tag X". This time, he stated, it was fixed and irrevocable. The date of the Venus Fleet landing was to be April 21, 1960! (Note how X-Day was set for one day after Hitler's birth month and day, April 20th)

April 21st arrived...underline{uneventfully}. Again for some unknown
reason the Venusian UFO fleet had seen fit to stay away. This
time, the failure of the Spaceships to "arrive" as Michalek had
promised, brought forth a storm of protesting letters from readers
of the "NEW EUROPE". The chart below shows the curve of Michalek's success and popularity from 1958 to May, 1960. It is based on the great number of letters from the public which have been
sent to the Editor of the "NEW EUROPE" newspaper.

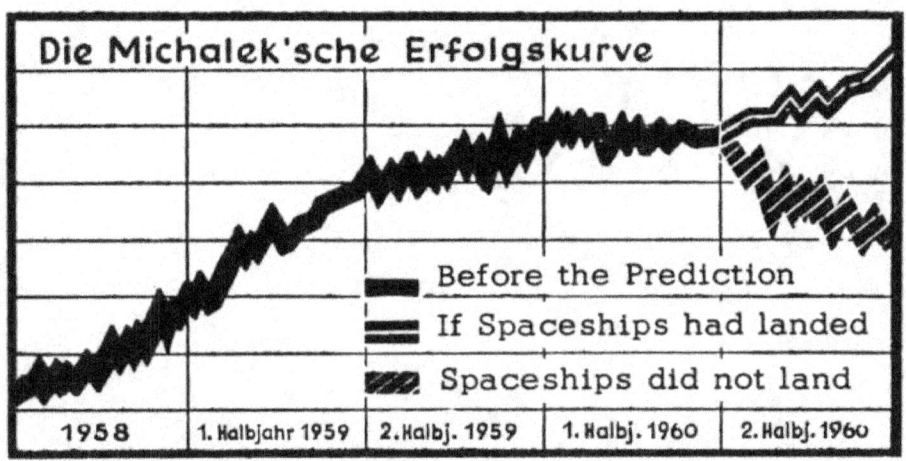

Die Michalek'sche Erfolgskurve

━━ Before the Prediction
━━ If Spaceships had landed
▧▧ Spaceships did not land

| 1958 | 1. Halbjahr 1959 | 2. Halbj. 1959 | 1. Halbj. 1960 | 2. Halbj. 1960 |

Notice how -- from 1958 to 1959 --Michalek's following in-
creased by leaps and bounds in all parts of the world. Member-
ship in his organization -- The Supreme World Republic -- grew
rapidly from a few hundred members to more than 30,000. From
the beginning of 1959 to April 21,1960, the curve of favor of Michalek's popularity went way up. But since April 21, 1960, a
noticeable decline toward the negative side has been observed,

Because the predicted Venus Landing didn't take place -- and
hasn't to the date of this writing -- the curve of Michalek's success has sunk into the negative realm, and Michalek has sunk
with it. INTERPOL in Austria takes a very dim view of his claims
and is opposed to him. Even Michalek's former staunch supporters, including the disillusioned Louis Emrich, have fallen away.

It is true that Karl Michalek's broken promises have left a
great many disillusioned and disappointed people, as the natural
aftermath of what many good Germans feel was a great fraud. In
your considered opinion, is Michalek just a naive "world reform-
er", a "harmless dreamer" or a real swindler in the grand style?

CHAPTER 6

UFO Surprise Package

◆

"FOR SOME TIME now, I have been the one designated to be President of the highest governmental authority of the coming World Republic. I have been so designated by the power of the Chief Leader of the planet Venus..."

The above words were the sentiments of Karl Michalek as he announced them to the world in a published message in 1959. If we look back a few short years in history to the year 1945, we discover a most significant fact:

Adolph Hitler was drawing up his "last will and testament". It was, in reality, his political will or party blueprint.

It appointed the next or forthcoming German Government. In this will, Hitler did not name a second Fuehrer to succeed him. He named Admiral Karl Doenitz as the next President of the Reich. Goebbels was named for the post of Reich Chancellor, and Martin Bormann was named the Party Minister.

Note this. The real power head of the Reich government is the Reich Chancellor. (Hitler's title) Joseph Goebbels was named Chancellor, but he was was eliminated by the Nazis at the end of the war, then the present true boss of the new Reich would be none other than...yes, you guessed it. Hitler himself.

The President, though, would be Admiral Karl Doenitz. It is possible that Karl Michalek is in actuality Karl Doenitz, and that his authority comes -- not from the Leader of the planet Venus -- but from Adolph Hitler and the Nazi Party.

Mind you, I say it is "possible". I do not claim it is the "gospel truth" or a proven certainty. No. It's a simple hypothesis

nothing more. So far Michalek has not "delivered the goods" in regard to his predictions of UFO landings, and his own broken promises have dubbed him a charlatan, a hoaxer on the grand scale. Those who formerly believed in him, now DO NOT.

My point is this. Is Michalek working with Hitler? If so, he is not kidding about the existence of UFO's. The Hitler group would have -- if my theory is correct -- a goodly number of bell-shaped, hat-shaped, and oval-shaped UFO's built by now.

Louis Emrich, whose personal faith in Michalek must have been badly shaken when Venus ships didn't land, had written:

"As has been explicitly assured by the authoritative side, there is not the slightest doubt about the reality of the Proclamation Program of Michalek's. The difficulties which have come up are mainly the fault of the inner organization. Several of the new members of Michalek's chief staff do not qualify to the requirements to the extent that had been expected of them. Furthermore, inner and outer political difficulties have come up which had not been calculated with..." (from the "NEW EUROPE")

WHO, I wonder, is "the authoritative side"? Might it be -- as we suspect -- the Nazi Party? Or is it Venus? May I submit that if it were really Venus as Michalek is claiming, there would be no such thing as "delays" in the landings. Any Space Fleet with a thousand or more years of experience in space flight would have no problem landing "on time" if they wanted to.

No, it is much more likely that Hitler has been hiding his UFO secret all along, since 1940 perhaps. It is quite conceivable that the Nazi High Command is still interested in world rulership, and expects to use the UFO's to enable it to achieve just that. The fifteen years since war's end is a long time. It is certainly a long enough duration of time to make many new plans.

The Michalek story may be a part of their plans...a preliminary test phase that for some reason, perhaps a good reason, had to be discontinued. If our hypothesis is right, Hitler has the UFO secret. And if we could manage to look in on his Argentine Hideout , we'd no doubt see quite an armada of earth-built UFO's. Not only that. It is also likely we'd find the craft well-armed.

30

But not with conventional weapons. No, we'd probably find the Hitler UFO's armed with ultra high-frequency electromagnetic beam devices capable of stalling any ordinary electrical system such as the ignition system of cars, trucks, planes, etc.

If those earth-made Nazi UFO's are built of secret metal alloys, they'd probably have to "import" certain metals from some other country. Logical one would be Brazil. It's right next door, and it's fabulously rich in metals such as tin, zinc, etc. This could account for the exceedingly high number of UFO sightings in Brazil. Those UFO's could be quietly transporting the needed metals out of Brazilian mines into the Patagonia stronghold.

Photo courtesy of Max. B. Miller.

In 1958 the above photograph was taken of a genuine UFO as it flew over Trinidad Island, which is just off Brazil. It was seen by the men aboard a navy survey ship who were taking part in IGY program explorations at the time. This may indeed be a Nazi UFO.

To the Brazilians and Argentinans, the sighting of UFO's is getting too commonplace to even comment on it anymore. During a recent 14 month period, no less than 149 sightings were officially reported in Brazil. Whole communities of hundreds of people sighted the objects at the same time!

Why were these UFO's often seen glowing bright red, orange, etc? Use of an "electrified system" for motive power. That produces an electromagnetic "forcefield" around the craft. Vikton schauberger, you will recall, invented such an engine in 1940. Electromagnetism creates a force-field in which certain energies developed in the process can begin to "incandesce" or glow.

In 1957 the saga of the "Flying Egg" began. On November 2 and 3 of that year, people in Levelland, western Texas, reported seeing a UFO shaped like an egg. It was about 200 feet long, and glowed brightly as though it was on fire. Most of the observers stated it was about 200 feet in the air when they saw it. The force-field of the UFO stalled motor cars on the highway.

On Nov. 5, Mr. J. Wolfe, a citizen of San Raphael, California, sighted the huge glowing oval-shaped UFO. It was sighted also by at least one woman resident of San Raphael. On the same day, the Coast Guard Cutter "Sebago" sighted a UFO resembling a "brilliant planet" moving at tremendous speed over the Gulf of Mexico.

On Nov. 5, Mr. Rheinhold Schmidt of Kearney, Nebraska, reported that he had "contacted" a strange, oval-shaped UFO near Kearney. Schmidt said his car engine went dead. He got out to see what was wrong and there was the UFO close by on the ground. He was invited inside the craft, and there met four men and one woman. They all spoke "English and High German". They told Schmidt they were from the planet Saturn.

On Nov. 9, at Weatherly High School in Lansford, Pa., the "Flying Egg" was seen in the sky by eight Junior High students who happened to be outside at the time. According to the children, the "oval-shaped thing" came down about as high as the rooftops. It rotated at a high speed, causing the four red lights on its rim to appear blurred. The students made a detailed sketch of it. We have reproduced the sketch for you on the next page.

On August 15, 1960 -- three years later -- the "flying Egg" was back again. This time it showed up at Red Bluff, California. The San Francisco Chronicle carried this bold headline : STATE COPS RACE 'FLYING SAUCER'. In reality, the strange object was NOT shaped like a 'saucer' at all. It was OVAL-SHAPED, just as the UFO was that had been seen in 1957. It looked the same and performed the same way.

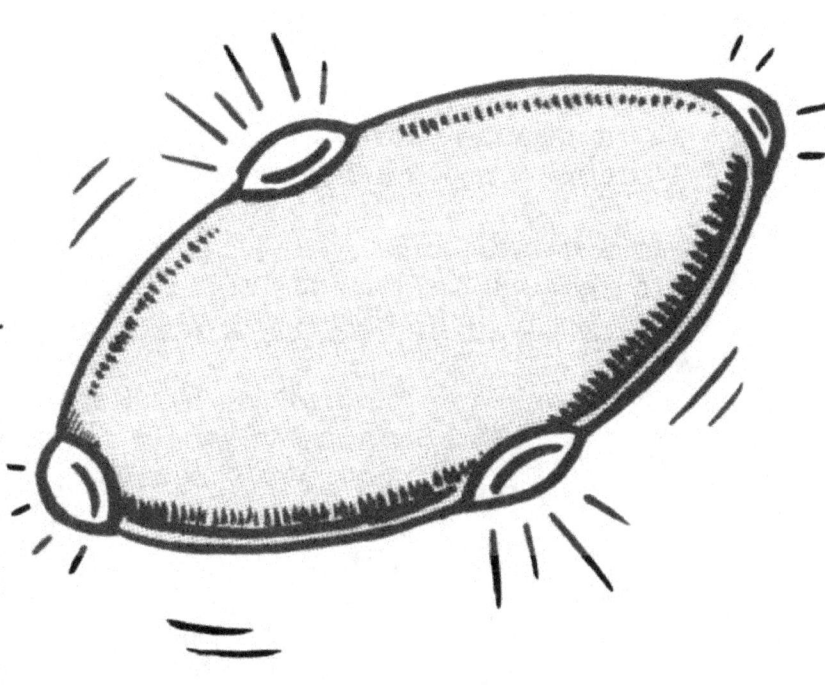

Briefly, here is what the SF newspaper said : "Red object sighted by Patrolmen. RED BLUFF, Aug. 15, 1960. A mysterious Flying Thing giving off a red glow has been sighted over the cattle country 18 miles south of here. It was as big as an airliner (about 100-200 ft in length) and shaped like a football. (oval) Sometimes it just hung silently in the air only 200 feet off the ground. (the UFO seen at Levelland, Texas acted the same way.)

If this "Flying Egg" UFO we have just been talking about is not "made on Mars", that is, if it isn't interplanetary --although we realize some UFO's do come from "outside" our planet --then what? Then perhaps it and a few other UFO's like it, was born right here on Earth, in the shelter of vast Patagonia!

C. Wright Mills, noted author of "The Power Elite", and more recently, "Listen, Yankee!", in writing briefly of Argentina said: "...armed men are in the pampas". I ask, "What are they doing there? Why isn't that fertile land being used for cattle and for ranchland as it ought to be? You and I don't need three guesses. Follow me closely. Is it not strange indeed that our man of mystery -- Michalek -- had released the following information :

"The scientists of Venus have learned to overcome completely the so-called law of gravitation. A certain proof of UFO landings is the fact that experts from Venus have been living here on this Earth for the last 15 years. THEY SPEAK ENGLISH AND GERMAN."

It is conceivable that Michalek is actually thinking of the Nazi UFO scientists of Patagonia, instead of true Venus people. It's been 15 years since the Nazis lost the war. Well-educated Nazis can speak in English, switch to German and then into Spanish!

Vice Adm. R. H. Hillenkoetter (Ret.) -- a former director of the CIA in America -- recently said that "behind the scenes, high-ranking Air Force officers are soberly concerned about the UFO's."

Why? Does the Air Force expect an "attack" or "invasion" of the Earth by UFO's from another planet? I don't think so. General Nathan Twining of the U.S. Air Force (Ret.) commented in 1954: "If they come from Mars and there is a world and a civilization that far ahead of us, I don't think we have anything to worry about."

I agree. But earth-built UFOS are a different matter entirely. What do you think would happen if a whole fleet of UFO's manned by earthlings from a secret place on Earth, were to actually make a "landing" in Berlin? Or in Washington, D.C.? What if they -- the pilots of the earth-built UFO's -- made use of "electro-magnetic" devices to cause all electrical power systems in those great cities to suddenly go completely, utterly DEAD?

Imagine it. All electrical systems in the cities "stalled" by the UFO devices. No electricity for lights, communications, or for anything else we ordinarily power with electric energy. Our military could not even send up its Nike guided missiles to intercept the UFO's, since they are fired electrically! Then a voice is heard in the air : Your city, your nation is helpless. We are here to bring a new way of life to this world. We ask you not to fear us, but to follow these instructions at once....!"

You take it from there. But don't panic. So far it is only "imaginary". God willing it will never happen. Remember, we are not talking about an "interplanetary invasion", but an earthly blitz by earthly UFO's. The real reason, perhaps, why the Air Force is "soberly concerned about the UFO's" right now.

34

CHAPTER 7

The Third Side — You !

◆

EVENTS HAPPENING on Earth, in the Earth and above Earth at this very moment certainly bear close watching. None of us desires to be caught short like the ostrich with his head in the sand.

ARGENTINA in particular, deserves our special attention from now on. The Nazi influence is active there, far more so than we Americans realize. And we have not seen the last of their UFO's.

Those earth-built UFO's are fabulous inventions. They can be turned into the greatest weapon mankind has ever seen... or they can be the true means of earthman's liberation from planetary bondage. Will those who have this secret -- and in this book we have reasoned that a Hidden Power in Argentina does have it -- will they use it to plunge us all into a third World War?

If we mean war as we've been accustomed to think of it, the answer is a positive no. Why not? Because war, under 20th Century conditions (atom bombs, super-gas warfare, biological and radiological warfare, etc.) is now a self-defeating enterprise. All-out war is ridiculous now and everybody knows it.

However, the subtle -- "nibble warfare" -- is not only quite feasible but workable. It is the artful technique of "nibbling" a chunk of somebody else's territory little by little, so it won't be noticed. It's a quiet invasion of a country by steady nibblers who pretty soon have moved in completely and taken things over. But it's so quiet and protracted you hardly know it's happening.

The real battle today is for the <u>minds</u> <u>and</u> <u>souls</u> <u>of</u> <u>men</u>, and the stakes are big -- all the earth and all the people on it. The fight itself revolves around one main issue. Will you and I keep our God-given right of <u>"Individualism"</u>, with all the liberty and

35

freedom that implies, or...will we sell-out our heritage for some illusory mess of pottage we'd get if we turn over all power to a totalitarian government or dictator? Who, among men, knows how to run your life for you with true wisdom from cradle to grave?

The simple object is this: to unite mankind everywhere in the spirit of true brotherly love, understanding and peace. To allow all men to be of active assistance and help to the total humanity on earth and elsewhere. To unite all human beings in a mighty, purposeful, indivisible body that will "outlaw" all that is detrimental to true progress of body, mind and soul.

FREE ENERGY, if released to this planet, could change things on earth as they have never been changed before. It could -- undoubtedly -- usher in a New Order of The Ages. Imagine it. A constant supply of free electric energy taken right from the atmosphere by everybody. Yes, a universal power such as Free-Energy could release man from many of the burdens now present in our world money systems. But who has such a secret?

The Nazis! If they have the original Vikton Schauberger "Electro-Magnetic" engine -- or improved versions of it -- they have Free-Energy. The UFO engine runs on power taken directly from the atmosphere. And that is quite inexhaustible.

I talked recently with a brilliant man from Europe. Holland, I believe, is his native land. It is, however, no effort for him to speak seven different languages fluently...including German. I asked him if he could give me any pertinent facts about the Nazis' use of Free-Energy, since I knew he had access to certain "inside information".

"Yes," my friend replied, "it is known that the Nazis have a Free-Energy motor, and used it in 1958 to propel a U-boat between Europe and Buenos Aires. It is also believed by many of us that there is an underwater station -- built by the Nazis -- somewhere in the Atlantic ocean between Germany and Argentina. A stopover place, no doubt, for Nazi subs and UFO's."

I thought to myself, amazing..simply amazing. I inquired,

"Just where are the Nazis, right now?"

36

"Everywhere. In all countries. Not only Patagonia, but the United States, Canada, Africa...and even in far-off <u>Antarctica</u>. The Nazi can never be content nor satisfied to just stop what he is working on. He must go ahead and achieve it. You must realize that the Nazi believes he is working for a New Age...the coming World Government that will benefit everyone."

I could understand that, even agree with it. What I forever refuse to go along with is the use of force and brutality and killings. Naturally, I had to ask him the big question.

"Do you think they will use the same old "storm trooper" methods -- violence, strongarm tactics, mass bloodshed -- to bring in their idea of a New Era in which man will be given the scientific keys to free energy, true space travel, and so forth?"

The Hollander smiled . "Negative minds might look at it that way, " he answered, "But we could take another viewpoint. We could imagine that the Nazis have learned, through past experience, that there is a limit -- a definite limit -- to the use of force destructively. Beyond a certain point, negative use of force has no value and becomes self-defeating to the user. They may have found, in passing far beyond the limits of orthodox science -- that all humanity is ONE, and must move upward together.

"It is my feeling," he said, "that within possibly the next five years, the Nazi leaders will suddenly return to the world scene and say : 'You have forgotten us but we are still here. We realize now that some thing we did in the past were wrong, and we are willing to make up for them. Our scientific secrets can open up new doors of UNLIMITED PROGRESS for all mankind. Here is what we have to offer all the people of the whole world...!"

Our discussion came to a close, and my learned friend departed. Alone again, I opened my Bible to Chapters 11 & 12 in the Book of Daniel. I'm glad I did. It clarified many world events, some have already happened and some which are due to happen. I urge you to read it too. Like Nostradamus, Daniel "saw true".

At this point I'm sensing your thought. "The Nazis -- will they <u>return</u> to our world scene in brilliantly glowing <u>UFO's</u>?" Our old friend, Michael Nostradamus, thought so. He wrote:

(1) They shall think to have seen the
        sun in the night,
(2) When the hog half a man shall be
        seen.
(3) Noise, singing, battles in the sky
        shall be perceived,
(4) And brute beasts shall be heard
        to speak.

The first line (1): refers to the brightly glowing or sun-like appearance of the Nazi UFO's when seen in the night sky.

The second line (2): could be naming Martin Bormann. A boar is also a "hog". Boar sounds the same as "Bor". Half of the concealed name is "man" or "mann". Result: Bormann. !

The third line (3): means that the Nazi UFO's will be challenged in the sky, no doubt by our national defense system if it is operable . Possibly outer space craft will play a part also.

The fourth line (4): I leave to you, dear reader, to interpret in your own way. Don't skip over it lightly. It's important. Yes my friend, you must use your own "6th Sense" as regards whom you will trust, and whom you will serve now and in the days ahead. I'll be at your side to help, if you need me. So will the Christ-minded beings of Venus and other planets. They too are saying "WE WANT YOU!" but only to guide and set you free.

We desire FREEDOM, not slavery. Because you and I have a vision, my friend. A vision that is real. We see Man of Earth coming into his true heritage of DIVINE LIBERTY wherein human beings transcend both hate and fear. This true approach to life may well be called the "RULE OF LOVE" on planet Earth. Love (higher spiritual appreciation) stands as the great "Balancer" between Brute Force on one side and Cold Intellect on the other. It is the Christ way. Every man shall one day walk this way.

Those who do not join a "hate" or a "fear" group may be in the minority -- increasingly so as time goes by. But if their Love, Courage and Wisdom is great they will have the HELP OF HEAVEN. This is my faith. And I believe it is also yours. It is up to us awaken this higher LOVE in the hearts of our brothers.

38

Our world, my friend, needs love. Not the sickly, soft brand of sentimental weakness, but deep understanding love. That's where you come in. Because if you're anything like me and the rest of my New Age friends, you don't believe in weakness.

Brutality, bloodshed and horror is not your "cup of tea" either. Like me, you are in search of a better way. Then just what is it that can stand up to the old, unnatural, inhumane "RULE OF FORCE" in our world? TRUTH. It alone can set us all free.

And the truth is that the "RULE OF LOVE" must begin to exert its divine sway in the present-day world right now or we may see this world transformed into another bloody bath again. This must not be. . . and you and I can do our part to prevent it.

A very wise man once asked me, "Michael, how many sides are there to a coin?"

I looked at the fifty-cent piece he was holding in his hand as he spoke. I replied that I saw two sides.

"Wrong," he said, "Besides the 'heads' side and the 'tails' side, there is a third side...the edge of the coin!"

Fascinated, I listened while he explained. "Few people are aware that there is a third side to every coin. Fewer still know that the third side is greater in a sense than either of the other two sides. Each of the two sides is bounded by the edge, is it not? In other words, the size or diameter of each side is LIMITED. It cannot go beyond that limit, right?"

"Right," I answered. Then he smiled.

"The third side which is the edge of the coin, is NOT BOUNDED by anything, it's unlimited. You could roll the coin on its edge forever (theoretically) and it would keep on going into infinity. The same thing is also true of Love!"

I never forgot that symbolic lesson. The Truth that you and I and a glorious legion of other awakened souls on earth and beyond it, have found the mystic "Third Side" of the coin. It is the "Christ-Love" within our hearts that shall redeem all of us.

****

 # Michael X Books

★★★★★★★★★★★★★★★★★★★★★★★★★★★★★★

1. "SECRETS OF HIGHER CONTACT"

Who are the Space People? How may you contact them? This book by Michael X reveals how mind-to-mind contacts are being made between higher space intelligences and "Contactees' on planet Earth. Most important, this book helps you answer the Big Question: Will You be a Contactee? You will learn about the Brothers of the Higher Arc, and how to contact them via your own Secret X. Michael X tells you what "X" signifies, and how to take the first step in "Higher Contact." Learn why your assistance is needed now by the Brothers, in unfolding a new phase of the Great Plan which the Space Brothers know and serve.

Only $2.00 postpaid

2. "THE D-DAY SEERS SPEAK"

In the exciting pages of this book you may find the most important message you may ever receive! Startling new information in this book gives you a clear picture of things to come soon! The "Seers" and "prophets" of our own times now give us a pre-vue of D-Day, the great Day when planet Earth gets its "Cosmic Housecleaning." Read what is foreseen by Ashtar, Frater VIII, Edgar Cayce, Teska, Oxtle of Mars, Michael X. Old Mother Shipton's ten NEW verses revealing an amazing vision of coming colossal changes! Learn about vital activities of the Space People, and the meaning of the "Purple Light." Here is priceless data!

Only $2.00 postpaid

3. "RAINBOW CITY AND THE INNER EARTH PEOPLE"

A fabulous city—"Rainbow City"—is said to be located beyond the South Pole, in Antarctica. Flying Saucers have been seen taking off and landing in this inaccessible region. Is Rainbow City a secret base for Spacecraft? Who are the Rainbow City people? Are they all from outer space, or could a master race of Inner Earthians be coming out from INSIDE the earth in Flying Saucers? In the land beyond the South Pole is a "strange great valley"—according to the radio message from Admiral Richard E. Byrd's plane in 1947. Does this ICELESS valley lead into the interior of the earth? **$2.00**

SPECIAL: The above 3 books if ordered at once only $5.00 postpaid!

4. "FLYING SAUCER REVELATIONS"

This thrilling book is for all students who desire to know more about our Space Friends, on all levels. Tells about visiting Spacemen from Venus, and other worlds. Michael X relates his first "contact," reveals valuable secrets of advanced beings. **$2.98 postpaid**

5. "YOUR D-DAY DESTINY"

Will the Earth suddenly—without warning—flip out of its regular pattern and "shake terribly" as the Bible predicts? When? What is the best preparation for D-Day? How are Flying Saucers related to the Coming Colossal Changes? **$2.98 postpaid**

 SPECIAL: The above 2 books if ordered at once only $5.00 postpaid!

---

6. "VENUSIAN HEALTH MAGIC"

In this book you discover the health wisdom of the Wise Ones! Space-Masters reveal a wealth of new, powerful and priceless information that may mean the transformation of your life. The magical Life-trons and how to use them. How the Wise Ones use Lifetrons to relieve human ills and injuries. What Modulation is and how it changes personal vibrations. New Age Foods for your New Age body. This knowledge is specially intended for all individuals who desire to banish poor health- **$5.00 postpaid**

7. "VENUSIAN SECRET-SCIENCE"

This big book is packed with exciting, important subjects: Communicating with Venus by Telethot and Menta-Vision, the Cosmic Plan of the Universe, the Secret-Science of Life, Love and Light on Venus. Its Seven thrilling chapters open wondrous new doors for you! Tells about your "graduation" from Earth to a wonderful new kind of world. Describes the magic life on Venus. Why Venus is called the "home of the gods." How Michael X contacts the Space People, via psychic stones. **$6.95 postpaid**

SPECIAL: The above 2 books if ordered at once only $8.95 postpaid!